She Knows

CHRISTOPHER BLYTHE BARTRAN

ISBN: 0692661360
ISBN-13: 13: 978-0692661369 (C B Bartram Books)

CONTENTS

Acknowledgments   i

1   Introduction   Pg 4

2   Chapter 2   Pg 5

3   Chapter 3   Pg 8

4   Chapter 4   Pg 13

4.2   Chapter 4.2   Pg 16

6   Chapter 6   Pg 26

7   Chapter 7   Pg 32

8   Chapter 8   Pg 36

9   Chapter 9   Pg 39

10   Chapter 10   Pg 43

PART 2

1   Chapter 1   Pg 48

2   Chapter 2   Pg 53

3   Chapter 3   Pg 60

4   Chapter 4   Pg 65

ACKNOWLEDGMENTS

Madeline E. Buhr / The Editor

DEDICATED

TO EVERY STRONG WOMAN

INTRODUCTION

It is said nothing is more dangerous than a woman who knows she is gorgeous. She holds power over those around her, those who will bend and melt away in her wake. It is also believed people do not know they are evil. People are doing what they believe to be correct, but only to other people's perspectives is the act deemed good or bad. How can you know one, but not the other? If a woman is smart enough to know the power she wields, why is it automatically assumed she would not be aware of the evil inside her? There is "evil" lurking inside all of us.

You may come back with a word like 'Conscience.' What do you think it is? What do you think of vampires with gelled hair styles and a humanity switch being desperate to take the cure for vampirism?

Not having a conscience is not a prerequisite to being evil; you can simply ignore it and turn it off, just like a switch.

CHAPTER 2

"Dear Journal,

As I write this entry today I fear what is to come. Today my friends Luke, Andrew, and Chris came round to ride on my 50cc motor bike in the pit. The pit was mined for whatever resource they could get out of the ground, leaving nothing left but a huge hole that eventually grassed over and became a huge pit. There is JCB tires laying around, that is the tires from a digger with a bucket on the back. We call them JCB's, as that is the company that owns them. The pit is a nice make-shift dirt track, perfect for my bike.

My friends I invited round, so I wouldn't be bored and so they could come to mess around on the motor bike. We won't be allowed to drive for another couple of years as we are only fourteen, so this will be the closest thing they will get to driving anything for now. However, the bike is not the reason they come. Not the whole reason at any rate, I know it. Oh there is some fools that doesn't even realized they been drugged into a stupor. One created not by liquor, but one created solely by my sister. She commands power over them, flirting just the right amount, never giving too much to one. Sometimes all it takes is her smiling and I catch my friends with the strangest smirk on their faces, happy that a girl would smile at them. The fools would do anything for her if she asked it, and yet, this is my sister. I suppose she is nice looking, nice as anyone's sister could be without it getting strange. It is supposed to be my role as big brother to protect her from the flies. Yet, I feel drawn to protect the flies from my own sister, as they have no idea of the situation they put themselves in.

In two years her powers will be let loose on the world and knowing my sister, Lynn, based now on how I seen her toy with the boys and girls, I cannot help but wonder what will happen when the world is her audience, not just the high school. I love my sister and I will defend her; I just cannot help but wonder if there is a limit even to brotherly love. Am I safe due to the fact of being brother and sister? Does this protect me or am I to be a victim of her prowess as well? I have no designs like my friends do, even if they don't realize it themselves yet. From an outsider's point of view, everything she does is so fluid and seems so natural that it is almost poetic, if it wasn't for the method behind the hidden motives. Year 9 of school, the second year of high school—in England, you go to ~~school~~ jail until you reach 16 years of age: beginning at age 4-5, and spending 3 years for first school, 5 for middle school, and 5 for high school. The system is set up like a production line; children from ages 4-5 get placed on the production line in first school and are processed at the end into what the government hopes to be educated citizens ready to enter into a work force. They teach you nothing about life. They teach you to count, how to tie your own shoes, how to read and write your name, but they do nothing to prepare you for life after school. Just like jail, you cannot escape. If you don't go, your parents go to jail, making sure in the minds of us children that going to school is a test of our family loyalty. Skipping school was jeopardizing your family safety, so in turn, by not going to school, you are betraying your own family. It is nothing like the American school system where they keep you until you're 18 and teach you what you need to know to be able to survive. Although, I hear there are designs to Americanize the school system: yearbooks, proms, even lockers. Ha! If we just had lockers, I would be happy, instead of having to carry a huge gym bag full of nothing but books, folders, science projects. It's enough weight and pressure that our shoulders looked like they are ripped. One of my classmates got a broken shoulder as he tried to carry his classmates' bags for a day. He wanted money and offered to carry their bags for the day for £5. He only got the 3rd bag on and we heard his right shoulder break. Needless to say, he won't be doing that again. But still, no lockers we were told, at least not until after our Year has left school.

So at the age of 16, regardless if you are ready or not, you have to take the General Certificate of Secondary Education exams, or GCSE's. Your entire life depends on these little grades; your future rests on some old fart grading your papers. And if he comes into work on a Monday morning like we all do, you know you're just going to be fucked. Because of that, instead of going to college and studying your course, you have to retake the GCSE's at college. Education is free here until you're 19, so they see if they fail you, it is not such a bad deal; you get two years to catch up. And that is just it, once you are behind, you will never ever catch up. The people around you will leave you behind. It isn't their fault, it is how the system works. If you want the job of your dreams once you leave school, it's everyone for themselves.

For 16 years, just like jail, you have someone telling you what to do, where to go, how to do it, when to shit, when to eat, how to sleep, when to do work at home. Then suddenly, they throw you out and leave you to fight against the wolves.

For 14 years of our 16, I've seen my sister's power grow, and how she saw people listened. Girls and boys gave everything to try to be her. She wasn't the stereotype where she was the glamour girl, obnoxious, standing out to make sure everyone noticed her; people noticed her just by looking and seeing her. She isn't a cheerleader; in fact, she hates that type. We have no cheerleaders or any sport teams that would need a cheerleader, unless you count girl's hockey, basketball teams, or the boy's soccer/Cricket team.

No, she was the perfect wolf in sheep's clothing. She blended in, never drawing attention to herself. First came the girls just wanting to be friends, and sure enough, she surrounded herself with them. Oh, I'm sure there was some she considered friends, however, she never considered them anything above a pet.

She made sure she did all school work that was assigned to her, making her untouchable by the staff. She never set a foot wrong, except for normal things girls go through that age, I suspect.

In Year 8, the first year of high school, one of the older girls from year 10, who was at least

5' 8", came storming up to Lynn, knocked her books out of her hands, and pushed and shoved her, trying to get her to fight back. It was masterful; Lynn just stood and shed one fake tear, which made her attacker over confident. Not noticing Mr. Wadlow, the assistant headmaster, behind her, the older girl went to hit my sister and he caught her fist just as she had started to swing.

Oddly enough, that same day, I saw my sister come out of the girl's bathroom in the south block, the block that held all the science labs. She had a red mess over her mouth and hands. I asked her if she was ok, but she simply told me it was an accident during science class.

An hour later, the bell sounded announcing us to the hall. The girl that had attacked my sister was found dead. They talked to my sister with our parents present, but in the end, they expelled one of her friends she had been friends with since our first school, Browick Road School. The older girl had died with a Bunsen burner focused on her throat.

Thinking about it now, you think it could have been…?

I'm sure it wasn't. She is my sister; she wouldn't do that… Although, it was funny seeing the trick she played on my friend today. He had been in love for a while, at least he knew it; I give him credit for being honest about it. He wanted me to speak to her for him. He wanted to do a trade, just a classic trade of you show me yours, I'll show you mine. My sister had her friends sitting next to her on the bed and I stood next to him.

He came in all serious and true to his word. He started off the trade and showed. Lol haha. And when it came to my sister's turn, she pulled out two socks… the look on his face.

I honestly think she would have given those American gangsters of the 1950's a run for their money. Still, that was not the only case of someone going missing or ending up dead. But this is my sister …

Could she really be the reas…

CHAPTER 3

"Did you kill him?" asked a woman's voice.

"Well, he has a hole through his head; I don't think it is possible to come back from that," Lynn replied sarcastically.

"How could you kill your own brother?" the original voice responded.

"You just saw how I killed him. Oh, you mean the fact he was my brother did not stop me from killing him?

"Well, you read what he was writing. If anyone else read that, they would get the wrong idea, just as my brother did. He was right about one thing. The fact that he was my brother protected him from falling in love with me like his friends, which made him dangerous. I made my father leave our mum, and just like his dad, I had to make sure John would not be a problem anymore." Lynn turned to leave the room, and as she did, she dropped the letter opener she had used to put a hole through the back of her brother's head.

"Oh dear, clumsy me," Lynn remarked. "Could you be kind enough to pick that up for me? My back is hurting me today; I can't bend over." She feigned, placing her left hand on the small of her back to express pain.

The woman picked up the letter opener and went to hand it to Lynn.

"Oh no, dear, please put it on the table over there," she said, pointing. As the woman went to set the letter opener down, Lynn took off her latex gloves. As she did, she looked down at her clothes and saw she was in her PJ's. Lynn and her friend were having a sleepover. Lynn and Samantha had been friends since their first year together at Robert Kett Middle School. She took off her sleeping top and dropped her pants on the floor. Naked, she ran back to her room with Samantha following close behind.

"Wait here, Samantha," Lynn ordered, as she ran into the bathroom and started to take a shower. She took some of the cleaning bleach and started to wash herself, ignoring the burning. However, being in the shower, the burn didn't last long.

Looking at the bathroom clock on the wall, she remarked, "Hmm, 7:30. Mum

will be awake soon." She turned the water off; her hands and forearms were red from the burning, but it didn't hurt at all. She had a plan for that.
She got out and put on a clean night gown. Stepping out of the bathroom, she returned to her room to find an anxious Samantha.

"What we going to do?" she pleaded.

"Did you do as I said?" Lynn responded.

"Yes, here is the entry he was working on. I placed the one I wrote on his desk instead," Samantha responded in earnest, as she placed the entry back into her dressing gown.

"Okay, good,"—Lynn smiled to herself—"so it is time." She suddenly grabbed Samantha by the shoulders, kissed her fully on the mouth, and pulled back.

"What was that for?" Samantha questioned with a puzzled look on her face. She was taken aback by the sudden PDA from Lynn.

"For being a friend." Instantly after saying that, Lynn spun on the spot and ran into her brother's room and screamed at the top of her voice. She screamed, and screamed, and screamed.

Her mother came running into her son, John's, room to see Lynn cradling her dead brother's body, still warm to the touch.

"Mum, call 999! Call for an ambulance," Lynn sobbed, her words unclear.

Samantha had already passed the point of being able to determine if Lynn was just doing a fine bit of acting or actually being sincere. She just stood and watched as Lynn's mother ran to the phone.

The police, although annoyed that the scene had been disturbed, waited for a doctor to come gently lift Lynn away and take her to her room. The doctor prescribed her a sedative. Samantha made some kind of gesture she would could but the police stopped her from leaving.

The Police Sergeant, Sergeant Wilkinson, stated that everyone was a witness. No one was allowed to leave until they had been questioned and until the police had salvaged what little they could from the crime scene.

"I don't understand. Witness for what? Is it not clear it is suicide, Sergeant?"

said the mum, still sobbing.

"Whatever this is, it is not suicide, ma'am. They did a piss poor job of making it look like a suicide." Then he quickly added, "Beg your pardon, ma'am." He realized he was accidentally being rude; he could talk like that to the people under his charge, but not to the civilians.

"How do you know?" the mum asked, as she gave Samantha an inquisitive look. "Besides John, only my daughter and her school friend and myself were here."

"We will look for any signs of forced entry, ma'am. However, if you forgive me, I'm afraid we have to follow protocol." He stood up, looked to one of his female constables, and waved for her to come to him.

"Do you consent, ma'am?" Sergeant Wilkinson asked. With forced politeness, she nodded, and the female constable proceeded to pat her down and began to search, not that she could hide much wearing her dressing gown.

"Sir, I will go put the kettle on, sir, to help for the shock," said a fellow constable. He had been jotting everything said down onto a note pad, as well as recording the conversation on a tape.

Sergeant Wilkinson nodded.

"I'll show you where the bags are, Constable," said Samantha, sounding a bit too nervous, and the Sergeant picked up on it.

"My dear, can you tell me what you and your friend were doing last night?"

Samantha didn't get to respond. Instead, Lynn's mum interjected, "Sergeant, you cannot ask anything without her parents present. I can assure you she was with my daughter all last night; I could hear them. Anything else, you need to wait for her parents."

"I have to question her in front of her parents, but I do not need yours or her parents' consent to do a search. Will you bare witness or would you like one of my constables to be witness?" the Sergeant replied with a rather frustrated tone. He thought to himself, 'Didn't she realize her son was killed? Why slow the progress down?'

She nodded. As she did, the female constable who searched her earlier went to do a light pat down on Samantha. "It's okay, dear. It be over really quick. Just something we have to do, you understand."

The constable, with both hands, felt the sides of Samantha's dressing gown, and found nothing. She felt along her stomach region and heard something crinkle.

"What is that, dear? List of boys you like and dislike?" the female constable asked, with a wink.

The constable reached in and pulled out the blood stained paper. "Sir!" she instantly shouted, looking aghast. She held the paper by the corner, between two fingertips, waiting until it could be placed in an evidence bag.

"Was it a love letter he was writing to you?" the female constable remarked, refusing to believe Samantha could be guilty of murder.

"What did you do?!" Lynn's mum shouted.

Samantha attempted to plead the paper wasn't hers, just as the Sargent stepped in.

"Too bloody right, it's not yours. I think for the time being you need to be taken into protective custody," Wilkinson stated, seeing the glare from the dead boy's mom.

Since Samantha was only 13 and she had yet to reach her 14th birthday, they didn't put cuffs on her and just escorted her to the car. The forensic team arrived soon. As they started to collect the evidence, including Lynn's pajamas, they found the weapon.

Sargent Wilkinson was convinced after no forced entry was discovered. He grew more confident about the person guilty of the crime, and he took them into protective custody.

The sister, Lynn, was covered in her brother's blood, but she was holding him as his people found the body. She had been in too much of a state, so the doctor blocked him from talking to Lynn for at least 48 hours. By the time, that deadline came and went, it grew less and less important to speak to her. They found the weapon used, covered with Samantha's prints, hidden in Lynn's pajamas. They believe it was an attempt to discredit Lynn and pin it on her as the murderer.

In the end, Samantha was sent to the sentence of Her majesty's pleasure. For children, this means going to a detention center until the Queen of England pardons you. On the day of Samantha's 18th birthday, she would be transferred to an adult jail.

The only thing that had puzzled Samantha was the note they had found on her was not the note she had originally taken from John. She just couldn't figure out how the one they found got into her dressing gown.

CHAPTER 4

"Dear Journal, as I write this entry today, I fear what is to come. Today, my friends Luke, Andrew and Chris came round to ride on my 50cc motor bike in the pit. The pit was mined for whatever resource they could get out of the ground, leaving nothing left but a huge hole that eventually grassed over and became a huge pit. There are JCB tires laying around, and a digger with a bucket on the back. We call them JCB's because that is the company that owns them, and the pit is a nice make-shift dirt track that is perfect for my bike.

My friends I invited round, so I wouldn't be bored and so they could come mess around on the motor bike. We won't be allowed to drive for another couple of years, as we are currently only fourteen. This will be the closest thing they will get to driving anything for now. However, the bike is not the reason they come, not the whole reason at any rate. I know it. Oh, there is some fools that don't even realize they been drugged into a stupor, one created not by liquor, but only by Samantha. She commands power over them and flirts just the right amount, never giving too much attention to one. Sometimes all it takes is her smiling. I catch my friends with the strangest smirk on their faces, happy that a girl would smile at them. The fools would do anything for her if she asked it. And yet, this is Samantha, my half sister. I suppose she is nice looking, as nice as anyone's sister could be without it getting strange. It is supposed to be my role as big brother to protect my sister, Lynn, from the flies. Yet I feel drawn to protect the flies from Samantha, as they have no idea of the situation they put themselves in.

In two years, her powers will be let loose on the world, and knowing Samantha, based now on how I seen her toy with the boys and girls, I cannot help but wonder what will happen when the world is her audience and not just the high school. I love my half-sister and I will defend her. I just cannot help but wonder, is there a limit to even brotherly love? Due to the fact of being brother and sister, does this protect me or am I to be a victim of her prowess as well? I have no designs like my friends do, even if they don't realize it themselves yet. From an outsider's point of view, everything she does is so fluid and seems so natural that it is almost poetic, if it wasn't for the method behind the hidden motives. Year 9 of school was the second year of high school. In England, you go to ~~school~~ jail for 16 years: 4 for first school, 4 for middle school, and 4 for high school. The system is set up like a production line. Children from ages 4 and 5 get placed on the production line in first school and are processed at the end into what the government hopes to be educated citizens, ready to enter into a work force. They teach you nothing about life; they teach you to count, how to tie your shoes, how to read and write your name, but nothing to prepare you for life after school. Just like jail, you cannot escape. If you don't go, your parents go to jail, thus testing the family loyalty of us children. Skipping school was jeopardizing your family safety, so in turn, by not going to school, you are betraying your own family. It is nothing like the American school system where they keep you until you're 18, and they teach you what you need to know to be able to survive. Although, I hear there is designs to Americanize the school system. Yearbooks, proms, even lockers... Ha! If we just had lockers I would be happy, instead of having to carry a huge gym bag full of nothing but books, folders, and science projects. It was enough weight and pressure that our shoulders looked like they were being ripped. One of my classmates got a broken shoulder as he tried to carry his classmate's bags for a day. He wanted money and offered to carry their bags for the day for £5. He only got the 3rd bag on and we heard his right shoulder break. Needless to say, he won't be doing that again. But still no lockers, we were told, at least not until after our Year has left school.

At the age of 16, regardless of if you are ready or not, you have to take the GCSE's. Your entire life depends on these little grades; your future rests on some old fart grading your papers. If he comes into work on a Monday morning, like we all do, you know you're just going to be fucked, and because of that, instead of going to college and studying your courses, you have to retake the GCSE's in college. Education is free here until you're 19, so they see that if they fail you it is not such a bad deal. You get two years to catch up, and that is just the thing, once you are behind, you will never ever catch up. The people around you will leave you behind. It isn't their fault, it is how the system works. If you want the job of your dreams once you leave school, it's everyone for themselves.

For 16 years, just like jail, you have someone telling you what to do, where to go, how to do it, when to shit, when to eat, how to sleep, when to do work at home, and so on. Then suddenly, they throw you out and leave you to fight against the wolves.

For 14 of our 16 years, I've seen my sister's power grow, how she saw people listened. Girls and boys would give everything to be her. She wasn't the stereotype glamour girl, obnoxious and standing out to make sure everyone noticed her. People noticed her just by looking and seeing her. She isn't a cheerleader. In fact, she hates that type. We have no cheerleaders at our school, or any sport teams that would need a cheerleader, unless you count girls hockey, the girls and boys basketball teams, or the boys soccer/ Cricket team.

No, Samantha was the perfect wolf in sheep's clothing. She blended in, never drawing attention to herself. First came the girls just wanting to be friends, and sure enough, she surrounded herself with them. Oh, I'm sure there was some she considered friends, but she never considered them anything above a pet.

She made sure she did all school work that was assigned to her, making her untouchable by the staff. She never set a foot wrong, except for normal things girls go through that age, I suspect.

In Year 8, the first year of high school, one of the older girls from year 10, who was at least 5' 8" tall, came storming up to her, knocked Samantha's books out of her hands and pushed her trying to get her to fight back. It was masterful. Samantha just stood and shed one fake tear which made her attacker over confident. Not noticing Mr. Wadlow, the assistant headmaster, behind her, the older girl went to hit my sister and he caught her fist just as she started to swing.

Oddly enough, that same day I saw my half-sister come out of the girls bathroom in the south block, the block that held all the science labs. She had a red mess over her mouth and hands… I asked her if she was okay, but she simply told me it was an accident during science class.

The bell sounded an hour later, announcing us to the hall. The girl that attacked my sister was found dead. They talked to Samantha with her parents present, but in the end, they expelled one of her friends that she'd been friends with since our first school, Browick Road school. The girl had died with a Bunsen burner focused on her throat.

Thinking about it now, you think it could have been…?

I'm sure it wasn't. She is Samantha, my half sister. She wouldn't do that… Although, it was funny seeing the trick she played on my friend today. He had been in love for a while, at least he knew it. I give him credit for being honest about it. He wanted me to speak to her about him wanting to do a trade, just a classic trade of "you show me yours, I'll show you mine." My sister had her friends sitting next to her on the bed and I stood next to him.

He came into the room all serious and true to his word. He started off the trade and showed. Lol… haha… When it came to my sister's turn, she pulled out two socks… the look on his face.

I honestly think she would have given those American gangsters of the 1950's a run for their money. Still, that was not the only case of someone going missing or ending up dead. But this is my sister …

Could she really be the reas…

CHAPTER 4.2

Down on the old Browick Road, there was a huge open play field called the Reck that the town used for playing soccer games. There were three huge areas where you could play three separate games of soccer, with two of the fields at regulation dimensions. There were also tennis courts and a smaller play area with a sand pit for the younger kids. The park had two swing sets, one for the 'older' kids, meaning thirteen to ninety nine years of age, and another smaller swing set for babies and toddlers.

The Reck was sandwiched in between two main roads. The main road, Browick Road, led to the first school, which used to be a combined boys and girls school during the Victorian era. The school was later split into two separate schools, where only boys attended one and only girls attended the other. The school looked like it still belonged in the Victorian age. The other road lead toward Lynn's and her mum's home. In between these two roads led down to the huge open area known as the Reck. During the time when Lynn had attended Browick Road School, there had been a huge "death" slide on the hill joining Browick Road down to the Reck. To say it scared the shit out of you every time you went down it would be an understatement. The drop was over twenty feet straight down before hitting the curve to slide off the end. You were lucky if you didn't topple over on the way down and crack your head open on the ground. Hence the name, "the death slide."

The normal posture to going down a slide is to be sitting upright, so as to go down it at an okay speed, neither too slow nor too fast. However, if you did that on this slide, you would have had to hold on to the sides to make sure you didn't fall. Then you would cut and burn your hands from friction and the joining sheets of metal. The only good choice was to lay down to cause less air resistance. To say you fired down the slide and shot off the bottom would be very accurate assessment. It was perfect for the adrenaline rush, if you wanted one, because despite the name and the hazards, there were plenty of people that enjoyed it. Though eventually the conservatives got their way. The mother of the one boy who did split his head open led to the slide being taken away and eventually the hill grassed over. Many people to this day still mourn the loss of that slide.

When not playing soccer, kids could go hide in the trees along the surrounding border to play hide and seek, or boys could take their girls into the woods for some alone time. Others would just sit on the grass and talk to their friends. Some just sat on the swings and attempted to swing the entire way around the bar overhead.

It was a cold windy June 1st in England's summer. Lynn was sitting on the swing just relaxing and wasting time playing solitaire on her iPhone until she heard a crowd of people up on Browick Road. It was her friends, people she knew from high school. She put her phone down and waved to the four of them. She saw Emily, Lauren, her sister Lorraine Cun, and Vicky, one of Lorraine's friends she didn't know very well.

"Where have you been? You've missed so much school!" Lorraine shouted. As she was coming down the hill, Lauren punched her left arm.

"She lost her brother, you fool," Lauren reprimanded her younger sister.

"I know that, I was just trying to be polite and nonchalant. Life must go on, you know," Lorraine defended herself.

"Never mind them. How you doing?" Emily asked. When they finally made their way down the hill, Emily came across to where Lynn was sitting and instantly pulled out a 20 pack of Marlboro menthols.

She opened the lid and pulled out four. Then she shook the box, jolting one more free, and offered it to Lynn.

"Thanks," Lynn said. She pulled out a rolled up piece of paper and the spare lighter she had in her left pocket.

"So you not coming back to school?" Vicky questioned.

"Not for this year, I've been given all the work I missed and I'm doing it from home. I don't have to go back until the next year starts," Lynn replied.

She finally found her lighter and lit one end of the rolled up piece of paper. Lynn proceeded to light her cigarette and passed the paper on to Emily for her to light her own.

"What is that on the other end?" Emily asked, noting the red stain as she passed the paper to Lauren.

"My brother's blood," Lynn responded. This made everyone freeze and stare at Lynn. "Don't let it go out before you start your smoke," Lynn insisted.

"What is it?" Emily demanded.

"A fake note Samantha tried to plant to make it look like I was the murderer. The police allowed me to keep it," Lynn lied, with a matter of fact tone.

She got up and walked down to Vicky to recover the paper. As she walked back over, she watched it burn all the way to ash before dropping it to the playground's hard mats, just before the wind blew out the remaining flame and swept away the pieces.

"What a little bitch… I just never knew Samantha would be capable of doing that. Do you know why?" Lauren asked.

"Yes, turns out they are, or were, brother and sister. Well, half-brother and sister. John found out and they never told us, Mum and I. We have the same dad, but John's mum was Samantha's mum," Lynn explained.

"So why kill him?" Lorraine inquired.

"They think because he was about to come clean to us, the letter he was writing that they caught on her. He described her as his half-sister and she was also responsible for the girl that picked on me in school, for killing her.

"Mr. Walker came round to speak to mum and I about John and myself. He said we didn't have to worry about school; I could take as long as I wanted. If I wanted, they were prepared to let me take the GCSE exams over the break, then just not go back to school at all.

"It's a very tempting offer; I know I could pass them easily I just do not know what I would do after," Lynn finished.

"School wouldn't be the same without you around," Lorraine stated.

"Yeah, she is right, but still, it is just two more years and we would be out," Lauren commented.

"What can you possibly learn in two years that you don't already know, Lynn?" Emily calmly asked. "If it was me, I would do it. You would have the extra time to plan. If you want further education, you get a two year head start over all of us. You could complete any four year college course for free!"

"Like she is thinking about college now," argued Vicky. "I would travel if I was her."

"Rubbish. Where would she go? To everyone else, she will be a 15 year old girl out of school, not old enough to smoke, not old enough to be with a boy," Lorraine countered. However, Lynn interrupted her

"No age limit has stopped me from being with any boy. I don't think it would start now. Besides, I can look 18 if I really wanted, we all could." She paused to take a choke on the cigarette in her hand. "I just don't know if I want to do it or where I would want to go. There is security in staying in school I don't have to think, everything is done for me."

"What would you do for money? Work?" Emily asked, with genuine concern.

"Don't you remember last month? We went up to the city on the bus with virtually no money. How did we get into the clubs?" Lynn asked her.

"Showing our tits to the bouncer," Emily stated simply.

"How did we get drinks?" Lynn asked next in a calm tone.

"Having the men get them for us," Lauren jumped and exclaimed. She had a smirk on her face from the memory of it.

"So you are planning on getting through life on the elbow of a man and flashing your junk at people? What happens if the bouncer is a woman?" argued Emily.

"Women are the same, show your tits and kiss them," Lynn countered. "They'll be too confused and concerned someone saw them, flattered and feeling good. You know how it feels to be kissed, right?"

"Sure, I've kissed boys lots of times. We all have." Emily looked towards the others receiving nods as confirmation.

"No, that is not it at all. Look you are all straight, right?" Lynn paused as everyone answered her question with a nod.

"Right then." She got up off the swing and stood in front of Lauren. Lauren sat on the third swing just looking at Lynn, wondering what she was going to do. The other girls were watching intensely as well.

Lynn slowly walked up first. When she was just about four steps away, she leaped forward, held Lauren's back tight, and gave her a full on passionate kiss. Stunned at first, Lauren made initial attempts to resist, but very quickly gave up fighting. She started to enjoy it as she held onto Lynn. It was a slow kiss with Lynn staring into Lauren's eyes. Lauren closed her eyes to better enjoy the kiss. Then suddenly it stopped as quickly as it had started.

"Quickly, without thinking, what's your name and where are you?" Lynn demanded.

"Wa, wait what?" Lauren stammered.

"I believe that proves my point. Even though she is a straight woman, there is being kissed and then there is being kissed passionately. Men do it all too harshly. If men ever developed kissing skills like that, we all would be at the mercy of their charms. However, as you see, soon as I stopped, Lauren was disoriented. She was into the kiss. She didn't notice I unclipped the front clasp to her bra," Lynn finished proudly, as she stepped away.

"What?!" Lauren quickly pulled her top and looked down to see it was true. The cups to her bra fell aside as the top holding them in place was pulled away for her to see the truth of Lynn words.

"Are you a lesbian?" Lorraine asked.

"No, just confident," Lynn replied. "How did it feel? Good, right?"

"You took me by surprise is all," Lauren responded hurriedly with a defensive tone.

"Yeah, but you soon relaxed and enjoyed it. We all saw you hugging her back," said Emily.

Before Emily could turn back to notice, Lynn repeated the experiment on Emily. Emily didn't even resist this time. By the look on Emily's face, it was over all too fast.

"Quick, without thinking, what is the day after tomorrow?" Lynn demanded, as she broke away.

"Wednesday," Emily guessed, which received a chuckle from the other girls.

"Today is Wednesday, silly," stated Vicky, laughing.

"How did you learn to do that?" Emily asked.

"I'm a woman; every woman knows, well, should know," Lynn responded as she sat back down. "So as you just experienced, I should be able to get by pretty well. Just a question of what I want to do."

"Why don't we head into town and show you how handy that skill is. You are hungry, right?" Lynn asked.

"Sure, I can eat" Emily replied as they all began to stand.

"Ok so we will get food from the Chippy, Big Fry, or do you prefer the other place?" Lorraine questioned.

"Big Fry makes better fish," Lauren answered for them.

"How we going to pay for it?" Vicky asked.

"Were you not paying attention?" Lynn answered Vicky's question, sounding annoyed.

"Sure, but you can't go around kissing everyone. It won't work," replied Vicky.

She didn't get an answer, just a stern silence as Lynn walked off with determination followed by the others. They got into Market Street, which had all the main shops: Woolworth's, three pubs: Cross Keys, White Heart, and Green Dragon, and Two Chippy's, not to mention the banks and a mini super market, as well as a one stop convenience store. They passed Woolworth's on their right as Lynn spotted Andrew and Luke.

Lynn pointed. "That is our meal ticket."

Vicky held her breath and didn't say anything, deciding to give her the benefit of doubt.

"Hey, boys!" Lynn winked and started flirting and batted her eyes. She rushed up and hugged them both. Lorraine and Lauren followed suit, smiling as much as they could without looking constipated.

"Hey, do you have any money?" Lynn asked. "Us girls are hungry."

"I've only got 2 quid," Luke said. Andrew stayed silent.

"That will do. Could you lend it to us? We will be very grateful, ...very grateful." Lynn unbuttoned the top three buttons of her shirt to allow them to see plenty of skin, just enough to get the hint across to the dumbest of boys.

"What are you even doing here?" Vicky asked aloud. Lynn shot her a furious look, as one of the boys started to respond.

"Just hanging around. We going to get something from the store for my mum, then head over to work on Luke's bike," Andrew said.

"You using your own money to buy groceries?" Lauren asked.

"No, Mum gave me a tenner." Andrew patted his pocket holding the money.

"You looking handsome today, Luke," Lorraine said with a flirty tone. Andrew was totally focused on how Lorraine was openly flirting with Luke in front him.

Suddenly he was caught off guard, as Lynn grabbed Andrew's face with both hands and started kissing him very passionately and forcefully. She pulled him to the bus stop outside of Big Fry, and Lorraine did the same with Luke. The other girls shielded them from anyone else seeing.

Lynn opened her shirt more so Andrew could see her bra, then grabbed his hands and placed them on her chest. Lorraine was rubbing Luke's inner thigh before she pulled down his fly and slid her hand inside to start stroking. Lynn resumed kissing as Andrew all too happy and content to play with Lynn's breasts. She undid Andrew's pants with her index finger and thumb from both hands while the other three fingers sneaked into Andrew's left pocket to retrieve the £10 note. She moved it to the inside of her own pocket without him even noticing. She stealthily stepped on the back of Emily's foot as a signal.

"Look out! There is people coming!" Emily exclaimed, right on queue. Lynn and Lorraine jumped up, and hurriedly left the boys where they sat.

"Thanks, boys," they both said with a wink.

The girls were already in Big Fry before the boys had a chance to stand up. Upon standing, both of their pants dropped to the ground, which quickly caught their attention. It would have looked like the two boys were alone together in the bus stop in the most awkward position, but they promptly did up their pants again before anyone noticed.

"Do you girls know what you want to eat?" Lynn asked. The other girls nodded. "Okay, I'm going to speak to my friend; he works here. Go ahead and order." She turned to look at the cook behind the counter. "Is Michael here? I wanted to see him. Is it ok if I go back?" she asked the cook boy. He was all too distracted to notice much and waved her back.

"Large size, fish, and I'll get a Coke please," Emily said.

"I'll get the same," Lauren stated.

"Can I get a sausage with mine?" Lorraine asked next.

"Didn't you get enough sausage outside?" asked Lauren. The girls all laughed.

"Haha, I'd hardly call that a sausage, more like a pea," Lorraine laughed. "I've never felt one so small before."

"Vicky, you ordering?" Emily questioned.

"Just extra-large chips please," Vicky replied quietly.

When they walked over to the cash register to pay, Lynn returned, followed by Michael. Lynn was wiping her mouth with something. As she approached with a smile across her face, the person who served the girls had requested the money, £8.63, and opened the till. Michael turned to the other person and whispered in his ear. While they were distracted, Lynn quickly took all the £20 notes from the cash register and closed the drawer.

"We all good? I paid already; I forgot I had some credit here from before," she said as she winked towards Michael.

All the girls turned around as Lynn walked up beside Vicky. "So now what do you think? We went from having no money to eating like Queens."

Lynn placed her arm around Vicky's shoulder. "Shall we sit up there?" She said, pointing to the town's main tourist attraction which had seating underneath.

The girls sat down and started to eat. By the time they were half way done, they noticed a police car, "Panda," stop in front of them. One of the officers was the female constable that remembered Lynn. "Hey'a love," she said, smiling.

"Have you girls been taking money?" the constable asked.

"Not us, Michael in Big Fry allowed me to use my credit to buy these." Lynn pointed to the half-eaten food.

"I'm afraid they reported a large amount of money went missing after you left that was there before you arrived. Also, another report stating you stole £10," the female constable stated, reading the notes from her notepad.

"Well, we wouldn't be sitting here if we had money like that," Lorraine replied.

"Please stand up and turn around. I will need to do a search," the officer stated.

They complied, as Lynn had signaled to them not to refuse.

Lynn was searched first and was done rather quickly. Then Emily, Lauren, and Lorraine were searched, and then Vicky…

"Care to explain, love?" the officer pulled out the twenties and one tenner.

"I don't know how that got in there… I didn't take it," Vicky pleaded.

The expressions of stark surprise on the other girls' faces convinced the officer they didn't know she had done it.

"Why Vicky, if you needed money, should of just asked," Lorraine said. "Are you in some sort of trouble?"

"She is now, love. Come on, I'm afraid you have to come with me. Your parents home?"–she started to escort Vicky to the car–"Hopefully they will be happy with just getting the money back and don't want to press charges."

As the car started to pull away, Lynn quietly smiled to herself as she sat down to continue to eat. "You just never know!" she exclaimed, shaking her head. Emily looked down at her with a suspecting look.

"Your work?" she asked, as she pointed.

"Oh no, I wouldn't be so sloppy," Lynn protested.

"So what where you doing with Michael in the back?" asked Lauren. It was

Lorraine who whispered the answer into her ear.

"Ooh! You didn't, did you?!" the question was out before her mind could catch-up, remembering she saw Lynn wiping her mouth as she came back.

"I've decided I will take the exams early. I'm done with school, the world will be at my mercy," Lynn stated proudly. All of the girls just stared at her as she continued to eat.

CHAPTER 6

"You are in a lot of trouble, love. You need to tell me what you know and explain why you took the money," the female constable reported.

They were in a small room dark with soundproof walls, a small wooden table with two chairs on either side, and another male police officer stood by the door. On one side of the table sat Vicky looking worried with her very furious looking mother. A recording device sat on the table, currently set to record.

"How serious is this? Should we be getting our lawyer?" Vicky's mom inquired.

"It all depends on Vicky, ma'am. It's her first offense. If she cooperates, all of this will be forgotten when she turns 18, otherwise it could lead to charges," the female constable explained.

"What you waiting for? Tell them what they want to know," Vicky's mom demanded. She was 5'4" tall with a medium build. She wasn't a heavy woman, but wasn't a slim fit either. She wore her winter jacket and her handbag sat on the table. She was quite frustrated, as she felt like the situation was a waste of time, just normal teenage trouble.

"Vicky?" the constable probed again.

"I didn't take the money... I don't know how it got in my pocket," Vicky pleaded once again.

"So you keep saying, love. So talk us through what you did when you left school," Sarah, the female constable, instructed. She had taken off her hat. They initially wanted to scare Vicky into talking, but she was still a child in the eyes of the law. Therefore, the majority of what was going on was just trying to understand the situation.

Behind the 4th wall, which held a mirror, Sergeant Wilkinson sat watching, sitting next to a child psychologist. He was a plump little man with a full mustache He smelled of horseradish which annoyed the Sergeant.

"She is telling the truth. She didn't take the money," stated Dr. Bodo, the psychologist.

"Then she needs to speak up," Wilkinson replied.

"… We had just sat down at the swings. Lynn lighted a piece of paper that had her brothers blood on it. She told us the police let her keep it. It was the note Samantha tried to frame her with," Vicky's voice sounded through the intercom.

Wilkinson snapped up, picked up the case file for John, and opened it. The note they found on Samantha was sitting on top. He quickly leaned forward pressing the button that activated the mic in the constable's ear.

"Constable, have her repeat that about the note," the Sergeant ordered.

"Vicky, tell me again, what did Lynn use to light the cigarettes?" she inquired.

"Are you deaf…?" Vicky's mum slapped her daughter's hand for being rude.

"She pulled out a rolled up piece of paper. Emily noticed the red stain on the other end; Lynn told us it was her brother's blood. It was the note that Samantha had on her that she tried to frame her with. She showed us how she can use people to get what she wants…"

"…and how is that?" Sarah, the constable, asked.

"You see, that is what I still don't understand. She told us every woman knows or should know. She kissed Lauren and then Emily," Vicky replied

"Does she like women?" Sarah asked next.

"She said she is just confident, she clearly not a lesbian?" Vicky answered..

"How do you know this?" replied Sarah.

"Because we went to get food, we had no money, and Lynn said she was going to show us how to use the skill. We saw Luke and Andrew in town. Lynn let Andrew feel her up and Lorraine took care of Luke. I don't know why they were doing it. Emily suddenly said someone was coming, but I didn't see anyone, and we all jumped up and ran into Big Fry.

"Lynn told us to order…" Again, she was interrupted.

"Lynn told you to order? But you had no money still?" Sarah questioned.

"Andrew told us he had money; I thought he had given her money his mum gave him, £10 to do shopping. However, when we went in she said she had a friend that worked there and she went behind to see him…"

"Who was that friend?" Constable Sarah interrupted.

"Michael," Vicky stated.

"You are sure?" Sarah pressed.

"Yes, I am. Why?" Vicky asked, looking puzzled.

"Go on, please. What next?" Sarah kept pushing.

"We ordered our food and then we saw Lynn coming out from the back, followed by Michael. She told us she had some credit and we were all good. Michael talked to the person at the cash register and we all left."

"That is all that happened?" Sarah asked.

"Oh, it may be nothing…" Vicky stammered.

"No, go on. Any detail cannot be overlooked," Sarah pressed.

"When Lynn came out she was wiping her mouth. She didn't confirm it, but we got the impression she was doing him a 'favor,'" Vicky stated, making air quotes with her hands.

"Please be clear for the tape. What do you mean by 'doing him a favor'?" Sarah demanded.

This caught Bodo's and Wilkinson's attention, causing them to sit up and listen closer.

Vicky looked towards her mum. "It's okat, Vicky. You will not get in trouble for speaking the truth. Sarah looked towards Vicky's mum, shaking her head to make her point clear.

Just then, the door opened, breaking the tension.

"I know you are not speaking to my client without proper consultation present." A tall man entered with his back to the mirror, blocking their view.

"They did not ask for a lawyer," Sarah protested.

"Hmm, I'm sure you didn't offer either. Regardless…" He walked over to the table and laid the paper work down. "This is to announce my presence onto this case. I have been hired to represent the accused here. Please leave us," demanded the lawyer.

With no choice the recorder was stopped and the officers left with the door closed behind them and the lawyer shut out the mirror.

"Sorry, Serg, didn't expect to be blocked for a small matter like this. Looks like a false claim from Big Fry," Sarah reported, sounding apologetic.

"Did she lie at any point, Doctor?" Wilkinson asked.

"There is no such thing as an honest criminal, and that girl never broke eye contact. She never shifted in her seat. She couldn't have been more honest," replied Bodo.

"Why did you have me confirm what she said about that paper? What does that have to do with theft?" Sarah asked.

"It doesn't. However, it told me the wrong person is sitting in jail for another case and the proof was reduced to ashes, which makes me wonder if this whole thing was set up just to rub it in our faces…"–the Sergeant let out a heavy sigh–"Cut the girl loose, no charges. Explain to her mother she didn't do anything wrong, she was set-up, but strongly advise her to stay away from her 'friends' and make some new ones."

The Sergeant walked by with his files in hand. He knew he had just been outsmarted and out maneuvered, and it pissed him off. Sarah, the constable, waited for the Sergeant to be out of ear shot before she let her hair out of its bun and shook it down to her shoulders to relax a little bit before putting her hat back on. Then she went back inside, leaving the door open behind her.

"Okay, Vicky… Ma'am, we're letting you go. The information you told us has been confirmed; we believe you were set-up. I strongly suggest you get some new friends, Vicky."

Meanwhile, Wilkinson had stormed off to his department upstairs on the 2nd floor of the station. He walked into the office where there were other plain clothes officers working at their desk writing up case notes, drinking tea, or eating. He walked up to the Captain's office and knocked on the door. Not waiting, he opened it to see his Captain and another officer sitting opposite each other.

"Sorry, Captain, just got back from the interrogation. Thought you should know, we got outplayed." He then closed the door again fairly hard and waited for the Captain in the adjoining room. A few moments later, a well-rounded middle-aged bald man came storming through the door.

"This better be good. What do you mean we got played? You were just supervising a theft."

"That 'John' case… we were set-up. The wrong person is sitting in juvi," said a frustrated Wilkinson.

"What evidence do you have?" the Captain ordered.

"The girl we just interviewed just stated on record that Lynn girl had a note with her brother's blood on it. It was the note found on Samantha; we apparently told her she could keep it. However, that note is here," he explained, holding it up.

"So where is this claimed 3rd note?" stated the Captain.

"Burnt. She used it to light their smokes," the Sergeant said, sounding defeated. He already knew where this was going.

"Then she got away with it. No one will believe one girl over the sister who was found cradling her dead brother's body."

"We HAVE TO DO something!" demanded Wilkinson

"Sure, get the bitch next time." The Captain put a hand on Wilkinson's shoulder in a sympathetic manner.

"But the girl is innocent!" the Sergeant protested. He refused to give up.

"Oh, wise up, Sergeant. Jail is full of people that is innocent. It's just a shame in her case, she is telling the truth and no way to prove it. It's done. Keep an eye on her; she will strike again."

The Captain made it almost all the way to his office when he was stopped again.

"Captain, the girl reported Lynn leaving from the backroom of Big Fry with a man named Michael, the person who reported the theft. She was seen leaving, suggesting she did more than just talk to him. Can we get a subpoena for the surveillance tapes?"

"Sure, if you want. If you discover anything, make sure you hand it over to the kiddie section. She's underage, so at least you will destroy a man's life. It would do nothing but paint the girl as a victim. She's a regular Moriarty."

"Sir?" asked a puzzled Wilkinson.

"Tut, how can you be in the police force and not know Moriarty? You know Professor Moriarty, Sherlock's nemesis." He opened his office door and leaned in before retracting his arm and throwing a book towards his Sergeant.

"Read it, Wilkinson. You've got a Moriarty, and she is all yours!" The only thing Wilkinson heard next was the sound of the Captain's door clicking shut.

He proceeded to sit down at his desk and start reading the book.

CHAPTER 7

"Has anyone heard from Vicky?" Lorraine asked.

"Forget that, did you hear they arrested that guy from Big Fry?" Emily countered.

The girls minus Lynn were gathered around a hexagon-shaped lunch room table in the main assembly hall of the school. The hall was an average size with a stage at one end, eight glass windows, and doors on one side facing the front of the school.

The hall was full with students and staff talking and eating, busily doing homework due for third period, or those who received homework in second period and wanted to get it done now.

Lorraine, Emily, and Lauren were together. It had been two weeks since they had gone to see Lynn. With only one more week before the school year ends on June 27th, everyone was ready for the break and discipline had started to fall away.

"What did he get arrested for?" Lorraine asked honestly.

"You really don't know?" Lauren commented. Astonishment filled both of the other girl's faces.

"You know what happened, right?" Emily asked.

"Yes, did he get arrested for wasting police time or something?" Lorraine remained confused by their expressions.

"Lorraine, you are being an idiot right now. We saw Lynn coming out of the back room; we know what she was doing with him," Lauren and Emily both said in unison.

"Yes, but it's not illegal, and there is no witnesses, only us… Oh." Now she got it.

"So Vicky told them?" Lorraine asked, though it was not really a question she needed answering.

"No, there is cameras in Big Fry. They would of checked the security feed. Lynn is not 16; its statutory rape," Emily stated.

"No, it isn't. They didn't do it. That only applies if they shagged," Lorraine defended herself, to which both girls just face palmed. Deciding to give up, Emily and Lauren got up, ready to leave.

Before turning to go, Emily turned to say one thing, "Forget about Vicky. She may not have turned him in, but she was bait. It will be dangerous if we stay around her, that is if we want to keep in Lynn's good books."

With that said, she was gone before anyone could say any kind of response. They exited the main hall into the lobby area where visitors were greeted to the school. At the main office, the girls all saw Lynn standing next to her mum at the reception office.

Lynn turned, saw them, and without acknowledgement, turned back to face the receptionist.

"Hi, Lynn," Lorraine as they passed.

Lynn turned and nodded, not saying a word. Lorraine noticed she had her left hand in her coat pocket, then no longer than 30 seconds later, Lorraine felt her phone vibrate.

"Who's messaging you now?" Emily asked.

Lorraine got the phone out, "It's Lynn. They've just handed in the forms so she can take the GCSE'S with the 11th graders. She will be at the Reck at 4:30." Her phone vibrated again. "Vicky ratted on Michael. She is dead to me," Lorraine read the message aloud.

"It's as I said, Vicky will have a target on her back now," Emily sighed.

The girls passed Mr. Wadlow as he headed towards the reception area to speak to Lynn and her mother.

"Mrs. Spoonman, pleasure to see you again. How are you, Lynn?" he said, as he shook hands Mrs. Spoonman.

"Thank you for doing this and for seeing us. This has been a great help, what with everything going on." Mrs. Spoonman was fairly tall, close to 6 feet. She was a well-built woman, the type that look more suited to drive a Chevy pick-up truck than a soccer-mum van, though she currently drove a van, as there wasn't really a need for a pick-up truck.

"We can go into my office and talk more. It is a fairly straight forward process; I just need to explain." He gestured with his right arm toward the direction where they should start walking and he followed behind.

It was just a short distance away. The reception area joined onto the hall way that had two double doors either side. This was the north block of the school. Mr. Wadlow's office was to the left, next door to the Sick Bay, which was a dark gloomy closet where sick students go and wait to be picked up. There are no school nurses here. Lynn suddenly thought back to her brother's note, he was properly right that it wouldn't hurt the English school system so much if they Americanized it. However, soon, very soon, school would be a thing of a past.

"So…" Mr Wadlow began, as they entered and he closed his office door. "Lynn took that A-level aptitude test and passed with an A grade. Also an Oxford standard entrance exam and got a 92.6%, which equals out to an A grade too, if you are not familiar with the American grade system.

"So we are more than happy to let Lynn take the final exams. She has missed three so far and will be allowed to make those up, if it is still what you want to do and if your mother is still consenting," he finished explaining.

"After everything that happened, I cannot return here for another year. It feels just so horribly wrong being here without my brother; everything reminds me of him and Michael taking advantage of me. I just need to get out of here. I just want to get it done and move on. I've applied for a student visa; I want to go study Psychology and Application Science," Lynn said excitedly.

Lynn's mom placed a sympathetic hand on her daughter's knee, and stated, "Yes, the doctor stressed it is important for her recovery that she be separated from the trauma and anything that is associated with it. Otherwise, she will not be able to heal or recover. She has vivid memories and dreams that she keeps re-living and the school has many triggers."

"Okay then…" he said, as he placed the form on the table and turned it around for Mrs. Spoonman to sign.

"Lynn, this is for you, the schedule for the exams. Your next one is the day after tomorrow. Because of the short notice, the examination board has decided to give you a 40 point handicap for the exams on just that day. Understood?" Mr Wadlow explained.

"Thank you, sir," Lynn said quietly.

The paper was signed, and Lynn noted,. "Sir, the police will need a copy of that form sent or faxed over, so they know I'm not skipping school."

"No problem, it will be done now. Please take care of yourself. I like to think our students go on to do good things, " he said, as he stood up.

He grasped Lynn's hand firmly and gave her a firm hand shake. "You were a good student. You have my most heartfelt sympathy for everything you've experienced and gone through, and I hope you get what you want out of life."

"Thank you, sir, I will," Lynn said, smiling.

CHAPTER 8
Time:16:30

"So what do you think the plan is?" Lauren questioned.

"We will know soon enough when we see Lynn," Emily answered, as they started to head down to the Reck.

"Looks like we are here first, I don't see her anywhere." Lorraine stated as she observed the area in front of her.

As they approached the center of the Reck, they noticed movement in the tree line. Then the the boys, Luke and Andrew, appeared. The girls just stood and waited as they started to approach.

"So you got here then?" Andrew asked.

"We are here to meet…" Emily started saying.

"To meet us, we know," Luke interrupted.

"No, to meet Lynn," Lorraine corrected him.

"Text her if you want, she told us to meet you here. You ready for the job?" Andrew asked again. Just then Chris walked out of the trees, not looking too happy and remaining silent, as he looked onto the scene.

"We don't know anything about a job. What you talking about?" Emily protested.

"Like I said, text her if you want." Andrew was growing increasingly frustrated. Emily pulled out her phone and began to text while Lorraine went over to Chris. She kept her back to the other two and hugged Chris tightly.

"You are not going to like this; you should leave before you guys get more involved in this," Chris whispered into her ear.

He glanced toward the tree line where the boys had appeared and Lorraine followed where his eyes led. She couldn't see exactly, but she could see what looked like a person laying on the ground.

"Lynn isn't texting back, I'm going to call her," Emily announced.

"Who is that?!" Lorraine insisted. When she caught him looking down, she shook Chris' shoulders to get his focus on her directly and no one or anywhere else.

"They won't tell me what it is going on, but Andrew is… well, liking it all too much. He took advantage of…"

"Of who…?" Lorraine demanded.

"Your friend," he said very quietly, not to be over heard. She spun on the spot with Chris' hand in hers.

With her other hand, she pulled out her phone and quickly texted Emily, who was standing just a few feet away. "It's Vicky in the trees."

Emily didn't even look up, but acted as if she was getting replies. "What she doing?" she replied to Lorraine's text.

"They had their fun with her." She looked directly at Emily now. Lauren Was just standing there looking bored.

"What is taking Lynn so long? Should I try calling her?" Lauren questioned.

"Go ahead, Lauren," Emily answered. "May be faster that way."

"Andrew, just tell us. She isn't answering me." Lauren gave up trying to contact Lynn.

"Well, you must have figured out that your friend tried to rat out Lynn. She wanted her punished; she wants you to beat her up," he stated matter-of-factly, like nothing was wrong with anything he just said.

"Well, that is all nice when said, but I don't exactly see her anywhere," Emily retorted. Then she discretely switched the camera on her phone on as she returned it to her pocket. At the same time, she sent one quick text, "999."

Lorraine pressed the numbers as she returned her phone to her pocket as well and let the phone dial from inside the pocket.

"Where is Vicky?" Lorraine demanded. "What have you done to her?"

"She's in there, I took my time with her," Andrew said, with a smile.

"Yeah, and being greedy about it too. You wouldn't share her," Luke said. "She told me to punish her; she didn't say you could punish the bitch. She should of known snitches get a baby," he laughed, followed by Luke.

"Why aren't you laughing?" Luke asked Chris, who was being shielded by Lorraine.

"They're armed, they got knifes," Chris whispered toward her. Then he stated aloud, "I don't think it is funny."

"Aww, you just saying that because she's there?" Andrew responded. "Okay, so as you told us, we punished her. Emily, now you can finish your job and finish beating her up."

Chris let go of Lorraine's hand and walked back into the tree line as he saw Vicky… She shuddered, then suddenly stopped moving.

"She needs to be punished for what she did," Luke announced. "So now complete what you started."

"There is no need… She's dead," Chris reported with a blunt tone. Just then four Panda cars arrived. Two of them sped up from the roadside access and drove over the field directly to them, while the other two blocked the hills so the boys couldn't run.

Chris had ran back to Lorraine. They all slowly backed away as the police approached and put the two boys in handcuffs, taking them into custody. Another group of officers gathered up the girls and Chris. They tried to separate Lorraine and Chris, but she insisted he was with them, so they just let it go. Simpler to just let it be for now than to argue.

CHAPTER 9

The airport taxi pulled up at the 'Departures' section of Gatwick International Airport. The rear passenger-side door opened up and Lynn's long legs set foot on the ground. Lynn's mother emerged from the other side and waited on the side walk while the driver opened the boot of the car to get Lynn's backpack and two suitcases. Lynn took the moment to stretch her legs, as she been sitting for the hour long ride. She was looking around to see all the taxis and people doing the same as her. She noticed a German family getting ready to return home.

Lynn could tell they were German. Well, maybe they were Dutch. She knew Holland used a mixture of German and French in their speech. She also saw four cars in a row pull up and leave just as fast as people in suits, on business trips no doubt, proceeded to enter the airport.

She felt her phone vibrate, as she noticed the last of the luggage was out and her mom was walking toward her. Lynn noticed who sent the texts and muted her phone.

"Who was that, dear? One of your friends?" her mum asked, trying to hold back tears. The wind of the passing vehicles was blowing their hair around.

"It's no one, Mum, nothing more important than this. I guess I really don' t need this anymore; I'll have to get a new one when I land." With that, she pulled the battery apart from the phone, and slipped the battery into her bag. She then took out the sim card and stomped on it with her foot. She could pick up a new mini-sim card when she landed stateside.

"Well, it's time. The taxi won't wait forever to take me back home. You stay safe, and you write to me all the time, everyday, okay? I'm serious," Lynn's mum demanded.

"It's okay, Mum. I'll let you know I'm still around. Who knows, I might find a dashing American man to look after me." Lynn knew she was tormenting her mum, and stopped when she saw the look on her mum's face. "I'm just kidding, Mum. I'll write every day. Promise," she finished, as her mum gave her a big bear hug before turning to leave.

Lynn's mum waited for the taxi driver to return with a push trolly. He helped Lynn load the luggage and she took over control. The backpack plus her carry-on were seated on the top shelf of the trolly.

With one last look at her mum, Lynn turned around and headed into the airport, not looking back.

She checked in easy enough and arranged for her three bags to be checked. The lady behind the counter greeted Lynn with a smile as she checked her passport.

"Vacation?" she asked.

"No, going to study in a college in America," Lynn replied.

"Oooh, very nice, dear," the lady said as she stamped the books and checked the tickets. "No return ticket?"

"I won't be needing one, I have a visa for studying," Lynn responded.

The woman looked at her with suspicion, "Just one moment, please." She got up and walked over to the supervisor. The man took a look at Lynn and walked over to her.

"Hello, ma'am. I understand you are flying to America today?" The man had short black hair and was wearing the airline uniform's AA sitting on his blazer pocket. Lynn looked for a name plate, but found none.

"Yes, I was granted a study visa by the U.S Embassy. I included it with my passport, but she was too busy being rude to me," she replied, sounding frustrated.

He looked down. "You gave this over with your passport to my colleague?" He picked up her passport, looked at the picture pad, scanned it with a blacklight to see the seal, and put it into the computer to read the chip.

"So how come you are not in school?" he inquired.

"I graduated early, which is why I'm going to school in America. I want a real education." She quickly glanced toward the original clerk, as she came up behind the supervisor.

"All of this was with my passport, if she had bothered to look, but she was too busy making a big deal out of nothing."–she glanced again–"I feel to make it up to me you should upgrade my seat to first class, at her expense." She looked directly at the supervisor, but could sense the steam coming out of the girl's ears, as that cost would almost equal a month's paycheck.

"Of course, Miss. I am sorry for the delay," he apologized, as he pressed on the keyboard to take back the original boarding pass. "Okay, Miss, here is your new seat, 66B. I made sure it is a window seat in first class."

"Thank you," Lynn responded, taking the pass. As she turned away, she could hear the two talking very loudly as he started to discipline his staff member.

Security was a breeze to walk through in comparison to the US border inspection, the waiting area before you board the plane. There were members of the airline and US Homeland Security. You had to have bathroom products in a clear bag, and they go through their papers to make sure you are not a terrorist.

It was a clear example of how crazy this country of England actually was. It was easier than cakewalk to get into the country, but leaving was a whole different story. It would seem no one wants the crazy English to leave.

"Hello, Miss, where is your parents?" a tall man at the checkpoint asked, with a Brooklyn accent.

"It is just me. I have a US study visa; graduated school early here and I wanted a real educations," she said, sensing if she buttered up the Americans she would get a more favorable response.

"So you are on your own? No one escorted you?" he questioned, looking back and forth between her and the passport.

"No, why?" Lynn asked sincerely.

"They are supposed to escort minors from check point onto the plane. I will make sure on the other end someone will escort you on the other side. It can be pretty scary the first time; I do see this is your first time traveling."

"It is," she responded.

"Where will you be staying?"

"At the college. I applied for Penn State and a couple of other colleges, but I got accepted into a college in New York state, the name of the school is in the paperwork.," she remarked, not even caring.

For some reason, this didn't bother Lynn so much as compared to earlier. This was this man's job: security, security of the people on the plane and of the country of America. How is he supposed to know who is or isn't a terrorist?

"Do these questions ever work to determine if someone is trying to do something bad or not?" she asked.

"Well, you just passed." He smiled as he returned her papers. "Take a seat, Miss. The plane will be boarding in 20 minutes. Yes, they do work," he answered, as Lynn passed by him and he started to usher the next person forward.

Lynn sat down in a chair and waited. She thought of what would be happening right now back at the old town that used to be her home. She smiled, knowing she would never be coming back here, if she could help it.

She pulled a book out and started to read, while a family with a small boy occupied the seats next to her, excited for their vacation. Then a young couple, probably in their early thirties, sat down preparing to return home, after what she suspected was their honeymoon by the way they were acting all lovey-dovey.

Why they would choose England was beyond her. Nonetheless, she tried to focus on her book. She was reading a great piece of fantasy, *A Breath of Fire*, written by the author Anna Courtney.

CHAPTER 10

Sergeant Wilkinson was overlooking the case file for the Vicky's murder. He stood in the observation room once again, looking through the mirrors. They had three interview rooms all being used at the same time, and he was listening to all three.

Andrew had been arrested for manslaughter. He was cooked. His lawyer was trying to work out a deal of some kind, not to get Andrew off, but to somehow to shorten the sentence. He was looking at pre-meditated manslaughter. The second boy, Luke, was being charged with Accessory to the fact.

However, the third boy, Chris, was cleared. The police found no evidence of his DNA left on Vicky's body and from what he told his constable, it seemed he had just been made to observe. Right now, the three rooms were being used to interview the girls. Lorraine and the other girls confirmed that Chris did nothing and was with them. They took Emily's phone and lifted the recording from it, which would be used to convict Andrew and Luke.

"So how you want to play this?" the Captain asked the Sergeant. The prosecutor was standing next to Wilkinson, looking at the file as well.

"What's got you thinking so much?" the Captain pressed..

"Moriarty," he sighed while rubbing his chin with his right hand. "It has her handy work all over this." He looked up to the Captain, "You think it was just by chance after we let the victim go home that she winds up dead and the 'friends' are involved here."

"It was Andrew," –Wilkinson pointed to him–"that reported the £10 stolen. Vicky told us about what happened in the back of Big Fry."

"So, you are trying to say this was a setup for revenge because of just £10? I find that hard to believe," the Captain replied.

"On it's own, yes, it would be a hard sell. However, not with everything else. We know Vicky was set-up for the theft; we know Samantha was framed. The connecting link here is Lynn. This was dealing with the boy who tried to get Lynn in trouble; this was punishment. I don't believe the murder was intentional. She wanted her friends taken care of, no loose ends."

"Can you prove that?" the prosecutor questioned. He was a tall man wearing a tailored suit, and had a black leather briefcase lying open on the desk.

"No, I can't. I had it checked; she was at Gatwick Airport at the time. She left in the airport taxi with her mom straight after they left the meeting at the school. They are letting her take the exams abroad at her new college," Wilkinson sighed.

"Then you have no case," the prosecutor stated. He closed his briefcase and turned to the Captain. "Proceed as is. Charge the first boy for manslaughter; we will charge him as an adult. Second boy, if he pleads out, we will offer six months and probation. Third boy, looks like he was just in the wrong place at the wrong time. If he is willing, we won't charge him with anything if he testifies."

"What about the girls?" the Captain asked.

"They never committed a crime. The girl died before they could… luckily for them." –he lifted the briefcase off the table–"Gather the witness statements, send them to my office, and I'll begin the trial preparation for the two boys. I shall expect the statements by 9:00am tomorrow." The prosecutor turned and left the room as soon as he finished speaking.

The Captain stood and walked over to one of the windows, "I think you should take some holiday time, Sergeant. I think our police force should start an exchange program with the American police force, don't you?"

"How long will I have?" Wilkinson asked, getting the hint.

"Your time and resources will be limited to the station you are assigned to and how long you can be accommodated for. However, if they make the arrest, it would be them that takes her to trial, not us over here. She has committed no crime here, none that we can pin on her. Go get the bitch, Wilkinson," he ordered, as he turned to look at his Sergeant.

~

"How long you going to keep us in here? We've gone through everything like six times already," Lorraine stated, sounding frustrated, as the officer recording the interview wanted to go over her statement again. The lawyer sitting next to Lorraine intervened.

"Yes, my client has cooperated fully, and presented no risk or hostile act towards your questioning. You will gain nothing new by re-questioning us with the exact same questions. If you proceed to do so, I will have to instruct my client to remain silent, so find another way to stall for time." This was the same lawyer that represented Vicky. Lorraine's parents, who were currently sitting in the back of the room, had no idea who contacted the lawyer or who paid him off, but regardless, they were mighty glad they had.

"I keep you here for as long as I want and you will stay until I'm satisfied I have everything I want and your… *client* is telling the truth," said the constable. He had black short shaved hair in a military style cut. His hat was off, sitting on the table next to the tape recorder. He turned to pace the floor once because the lawyer was right, he was playing for time and he had run out of tactics to play.

He briefly looked towards the mirror and scratched the ear lobe on his right ear. This was the signal, should anyone be watching, that he needed more information, or this interview would be coming to halt very soon.

He returned to the table. "Okay, I want to make sure of two things where your answers changed…" he began, and as if by magic, the female constable came in the door and stood with it open.

"Sorry to interrupt. However, you are free to go. We will no longer need you for any more questions. You are very lucky, Lorraine. Your friend, Chris, is going to testify against the other boy, which gives you a ticket out. You and your friends," the female constable explained.

Lorraine turned, asking, "What will happen to Luke and… Andrew?"

"That will be up to the judge," the female constable stated bluntly.

After 30 minutes of paper work and the parents of the other girls grumbling that they been kept for so long, Emily, Lorraine and Louise were grouped up by themselves.

"They questioned me for ages," Louise stated.

"That is hardly a surprise; we are involved in a murder… Poor Vicky," Lorraine sighed and bowed her head.

"I had the female officer that arrested Vicky. She thinks Lynn has something to do with this. Funny how we got the text to go to the Reck, but she doesn't show up. And it turns out she left the country, so she had no intention of showing up," Emily declared.

"So what does that even mean anyway?" Lorraine asked.

"You heard Andrew. He expected us to finish Vicky. He had his instructions too…"

"Get to the point!" Lorraine interrupted. "I'm tired and hungry, just tell us."

"We were set-up; Lynn tried to get rid of us," Emily finished explaining, as her parents came to get her. They were the first to finish signing everything, so they were allowed to go home first. Emily followed her parents and waved goodbye to Louise and Lorraine.

Part 2
USA

CHAPTER 1

The heavy sound of... *air, was it?* ...was whipping all around the city. Trash was being blown about the streets; the sound of sirens, car horns, and people screaming in their apartments filled the atmosphere. There were the echoes of people arguing, fighting, more car horns, laughter... and then there was the smell. Of all things, the city's aroma filled Lynn's nostrils as she poked her head out her hotel window and took in the atmosphere that was New York. She'd heard it was kind of difficult to not feel a sort of drunken sensation when experiencing New York for the first time. No other city could ever feel the same as New York City. It had been a couple of weeks since she flew to America, and she had some free time on her hands. Lynn completed most of the course exams she had to take for the GCSE's, and it wouldn't be until September for the term to start for her new college courses. It was all too clear; she was much younger than everyone else who would be attending the college.

In the meantime, she was given a chance to explore New York City. The college awarded her a two week stay at the Lexington Hotel at the corner of Lexington Ave and 48th St. The college sent a guide to accompany her and to make sure she was safe, considering that she was still quite young at just 14 years of age. The guide the college sent was a woman with long hair down to her shoulders, standing 5'9" tall and towering over Lynn. She wore make-up at just the perfect balance too, so it was respectful and enhanced the features of the face, but did not appear tacky. The woman was born and raised in NYC, and therefore spoke with a thick accent from the Bronx.

It was 8:00am when Lynn finally came down to the ground floor. She exited the elevator and turned left to head into the hotel's adjoining restaurant, Raffles Bistro. The hotel doesn't have its own restaurant as most hotels would; however, they had this little business serving double duty as a restaurant for the hotel and as a business for itself. If the hotel were to close, this restaurant would still be there. As a guest, you also had the choice of going to Starbucks instead, as its entrance stood right next to the entrance of the restaurant. If you didn't want a full meal, you could, in turn, get a light breakfast and pass through Starbucks onto the city streets.

As Lynn entered the restaurant, she saw her guide and walked straight over to her. She sat down opposite her as a waitress, a tall lady named Maryika, came and provided her the menu. The waitress asked Lynn what she would like to drink in a strong Russian accent, which surprised Lynn as she expected another New York accent. After she choosing her drink, she turned to her guide.

"Is there a lot of people like me in this city?" Lynn asked, just as a group of French cyclists entered from the street side entrance and parked their bikes along the side of the counter, taking Lynn's interest away from the conversation she just barely started. Maryika then returned with Lynn's coffee and asked Lynn what she would like to eat.

"French toast, please," she requested. Maryika made a note of Lynn's order, smiled, and walked off to enter it into the kitchen system. Finally, she resumed the conversation that had been interrupted after the first word.

"I trust you've seen your answer," the guide responded. "New York City is a city shared with the world. Many come here to visit; many come here in hopes of completing their hopes and dreams. You are one of the few that have chosen to come here to learn," she said in her Bronx accent.

"I'm sorry," Lynn began, "I forgot what your name is...?"

"I am Ann," the woman replied. "It's okay, I'm hopeless with names too. And we did get in late last night. So... what would you like to do here? We could spend a month here and not uncover half of the city's secrets. You may have heard New York is a city that never sleeps, which is true. There is two entirely different lives being had in this city, one by day and one by night. The night life is unmistakable, one of the wonders to this city, whereas the day to day life obscures and keeps hidden the secrets of the night before." She had smile on her face, which gave Lynn the impression Ann was having flashbacks of fond memories.

"Well," Lynn was about to respond. However, Maryika arrived with her food. "Thank you," she said to the waitress.

"Enjoy!" Maryika replied with a smile and walked away.

Lynn covered her food with syrup, cut a piece, and placed it in her mouth. Instantly, she closed her eyes at the pure delight and explosion of flavor in her mouth.

"Oh my god, these are great!" Lynn exclaimed.

"Have you never had French toast before?" Ann chuckled, unable to help herself.

"No, apparently not. Nothing compared to this! So much flavor. Doesn't taste like cardboard, unlike what I had back in England," Lynn said, after wiping her mouth with a napkin. "No wonder a lot of people are overweight here. With food like this, I would be too," Lynn stated, laughing.

"I guess that is why everyone over there is so thin then, because it tastes like cardboard," Ann replied with a smile. "So you were saying?"

"Well, I don't want to look..."–she paused to look at herself–"English anymore. I wondered if you could guide me in New York fashion."

"You sure you don't want a I Heart NYC T-shirt, or a Hard Rock Café T-shirt? Would look very good on you," Ann smiled, mocking Lynn.

"Oh no, if there is anything I noticed in the short time I have been here, it's tourists stand out, and they are targets. I want to blend in with everyone else here and just be, well, like you, and not like..." Lynn nodded to the French cyclists.

"You learn quick, maybe you will survive New York intact. Well, when you are done with your food, I know the perfect place we can go. I will let you enjoy your breakfast while I go back to my room and get things organized. It's 8:30am now. Shops open at 9:00am, but they are not at their best until 10:00am, so I suggest we leave here at 9:30am. Give you time to digest your food," Ann finished. She smiled, seeing the look on Lynn's face as she just shoveled another fork full of French toast into her mouth.

~

Wilkinson walked up the steps to enter the Midtown North Precinct. He walked up to the Sergeant at the desk, displayed his British Police Force badge, and presented his transfer and exchange papers. "Where do I report, Sergeant?"

"You get that badge from Toys 'R' Us then?"–the Sergeant looked up at him–"Just pulling your leg up there," he laughed. "Good to see you people want to learn from the best," he said with a beaming smile. "Okay, sir, please take this New York badge and proceed to your Captain, Captain Howard. Third floor, second door on your right. He is in charge of the

Crimes Division. Handles manslaughter, murder, things of that sort."

"Thanks, Sergeant." Wilkinson took his papers and new badge, clipped the badge to his shirt, and proceeded to the elevator to ride up to the third floor as instructed.

"Here he is, our own Sherlock Holmes from England, to show us how it's done," a voice announced as the elevator door opened, revealing five people waiting around the elevator entrance to the elevator. Wilkinson stepped out of the elevator.

Captain Howard stepped forward and shook his hand, "Welcome, welcome. Let me introduce you to everyone." Howard put an arm around Wilkinson's shoulder to direct his attention.

"We have Detectives Fable, Tina, Sarah. Then, we have researchers over in that office; you can meet them later. We have two other people currently out in the field. We have Behun here, our tech wizard, and our Fed liaison, Agent Patryk," the Captain finished, as Wilkinson shook hands with everyone.

Leading him, Captain Howard pointed, "Over here is your desk. Now, your C/O in England explained what is going on. You have someone that you say is 'colder than liquid nitrogen and slippery as oil,' that the target is now over here and that is your reason for the exchange. While I understand the urge to get your guy, you will be expected to work with us to maintain cases that we have here too. However, the department will help you. Now, tell us about this, what you call your 'target'?" Captain Howard asked.

"May I use your board, sir?" Wilkinson asked, pointing to the white board.

"Call me Cap or Captain. No need for sir, unless higher ups are here. Go ahead," Howard replied.

Wilkinson walked over to the board, opened his case files, and placed a picture of Lynn on the board. He then grabbed one of the markers.

"Okay, here is the situation. Our target was dubbed, by my captain, as a 'Moriarty.'"–he paused to write the name–"The target is female. She's 14. Very manipulative. Her name is Lynn Spoonman, and despite her age, she has pulled off some impressive stunts and managed to get away with them."

The detectives started to laugh and joke, as if wondering if Wilkinson was pulling their leg. The Captain, while staying silent, didn't look convinced, when the sergeant from downstairs nocked on the door.

"Sorry, Captain. Postcard arrived for our exchange student, just came by USPS." He handed it off to Captain Howard.

He turned it over and read. "Detective, you said her name is Lynn, correct?"

"Yes, sir… err, Captain," Wilkinson corrected himself mid-sentence.

"Your 'Moriarty' has sent you a postcard welcoming you to New York." This turned the laughs into stunned silence as they all stared at the postcard.

CHAPTER 2

At 9 Prince St was a store with a blue entrance containing four glass window panes on either side of the door. The design highlighted everything inside the shop, making it stand out so much that even down towards the end of the block, you could see the magical creations and makeovers being performed inside.

Inside, the ceiling and walls were solid white. Multiple shelves and counters for the staff stood atop wood panel flooring. There were mini islands stationed around the shop floor for the customers to come in and have their transformations begin. This was the Credo beauty shop, and this was the first place Ann, Lynn's guide, took her.

"I got appointments here for us both at 9:50am, so they should be just warming up. The first thing any woman must do is look after herself. No amount of clothing will help without the proper…erm," Ann paused, looking puzzled as if searching for an adequate word.

"Camouflage," Lynn said with a smile.

"Right! Camouflage. You're absolutely right. Allows us to blend in and stand out all at the same time in the right situation." Ann held the door open for Lynn to enter.

As soon as they entered, the girl at the counter spotted them and charged toward Ann.

"Ann, it is so good to see you again! And who is your friend?" The girl looked like she was eighteen, with flawless skin and no split ends in her hair, and no… no sign of any extensions. The eyelashes were fake, but Lynn couldn't tell where the real lashes ended and the fake ones began. She noticed the nails too, and although they bore very impressive designs, she could not tell if they were fake too or not.

This girl had black hair down to her shoulders with spring-like curls at the ends. She spoke with a New York accent. She wore a thin black lace tank top that looked so delicate it might tear at a light touch. A small jacket hung over top of the tank top. It was impossible to close the jacket's front, as it was just there to ensure your attention was focused solely on the midsection of her body. It drew one's attention exactly where the designer intended, so as to notice you are gazing upon a woman.

Below was frilly white cotton skirt that fell just above the knees, not slutty, but not too granny looking either. It was perfect. The entire outfit was a perfect balance to suggest a normal woman, not like the typical stuff that is too revealing and fashioned for sex. However, she was wearing basic flat shoes, which clearly did not match the ensemble.

"This is Lynn. She is studying at our college. She is from England and she is only fourteen, already graduated high school," Ann began explaining.

"What is it? What have you noticed, Lynn?" the girl interrupted Ann, sounding eager as a kid asking their parent reveal a surprise.

"Your shoes, and your feet," Lynn pointed.

"Yes, what about them?" the girl asked, not giving anything away.

"Your entire outfit is perfect, perfectly balanced and coordinated, down to your hair and nails. But yet, your feet show the outlines you normally wear, like you have worn high-heel shoes regularly, but the shoes you have on now don't match at all…" Lynn paused.

"Is that all you noticed?" the shop girl asked insistently.

It was all she had noticed until she had asked, which made Lynn look again, and this time, she glanced between the girl's two feet.

"You used to be a catwalk model, but your left foot is out of shape, so I guess you broke your left foot and that ended your career as a catwalk model early," Lynn finished.

Ann looked down to the woman's feet and back up between Lynn and the woman.

"Right you are, my dear." She came over to Lynn and held her hand. "My name is Lola. I am twenty-two. I used to be into fashion and did all the fashion performances here in New York, until I broke my foot. Besides, working in a store twelve hours a day, my foot never fully healed up and I could never wear the high heel shoes I love so much again. That is where I learned how to do the make-up that I offer people today. You better watch this one, Ann. She is a natural; she has the gift. She knows."

"She knows what?" Ann asked. Puzzled, she now wondered if bringing Lynn here was the right thing to do after all.

"Show her, Lynn," Lola said, nodding confirmation.

After making double sure of what Lola meant, Lynn walked straight up to Ann, led her over to one of the chairs to get her to sit down, and kissed her passionately for a moment. Ann was stunned, and just like Lynn's friends in England, just as Ann was getting into it, it was over.

"Wha…, what? What was that for?" Ann asked after getting a grip of herself.

"A weapon of a woman with confidence, one of many when she knows. Where is your wallet?" Lola asked.

Instantly, Ann stood up. Her pants fell down around her ankles, and her two bra straps fell out of her top. Lynn stood there holding Ann's wallet waiting to give it back to her once she had redressed herself.

"You see, Ann, to girls and women like our friend Lynn here, this store is to her as a auto store is to a car mechanic.

"It's her armory. She knows she can manipulate and control anyone she wants. She has the confidence, she has great observation, and she can distract, clearly. And there is a lot more she could do if she learned. Make-up can provide her the best ammunition to manipulate any target she desires, but it is only one part. Clothing is the second part. Make-up is not just for the romantic nature to lure the person you want. It can be used in many ways.

"Come, the day is wasting. Ann take a seat there please. My assistant will be with you. Lynn, I'm going to give you the Lash Application with Monroe Lashes, Brow and Lip Wax, and the Bridal Makeup. It's all free if you agree to come back and let me train you." Lola held out her hand toward the empty chair she was waiting for Lynn to take.

Lynn did not hesitate. She walked straight up, turned around, and sat down in the seat. She felt fairly certain she could get in and out of night clubs and make herself look eighteen or older, but she knew what Lola had meant. She would be foolish to think she was the only person like that. She jumped at the chance, and felt somewhat welcomed in knowing there was someone else like her.

"Ann, did you mail out that postcard the other day?" Lynn asked as she settled herself.

"Yes, I did. Who was it to? If you don't mind me asking. Was kind of odd sending a postcard to someone already in New York. Sorry, I had to look at the address to get the correct postage, as I almost asked for airmail," Ann replied.

"Oh, that is okay. It was to someone from back home that I know followed me here. I played a game just before I left and the game has now carried on over to here. I wanted to spike the game a little into my friend, as he didn't know that I knew he followed me here," Lynn answered, as Lola smiled at her.

"What kind of game?" Ann asked. Lynn decided it was best to ignore that question for a while.

"So in regards to clothes, I always love shopping at Topshop. Is there one nearby?" Lynn asked.

"Oh, yes, there is. It is on the corner of 49th Street and 5th Avenue. We can go after we are done here," Ann replied.

"I'll make the booking for your personal shopping, Lynn. I'll let the manager know you are a personal friend of mine; she will take care of you," Lola stated, as she started to prep Lynn for the Brow and Lip Wax before doing the Lash Application.

At 13:00, it was time for them to leave and head over to Topshop. Lynn exited Credo looking like a completely different person than who had entered earlier that morning. Instead of taking a taxi, Lola had arranged for a car from Topshop to come pick them up.

It took them forty minutes to get across from Prince Street to 5th Avenue due to the heavy traffic of the city. When the car came to a stop, Lynn saw two door persons standing outside of Topshop dressed in red velvet coats with gold trimmings, pants down to their boots, white gloves, and officer hats. The female door person opened the car door, while the 2nd door person offered a hand to help Lynn, and then Ann, out of the car.

Once out of the car, the door persons escorted them to the front of the store. The store was surrounded with glass windows revealing posters and models displaying outfits. Clear glass windows spanned above the first floor and all the way around the corner, displaying hundreds of model, both male and female, wearing a wide variety of outfits.

Two large US flags flew proudly from the front of the building. The eight story building stood tall on 5th Avenue amidst the hustle and bustle of traffic and life in New York City.

As the door persons opened the door for Ann and Lynn to enter the store, two of the Topshop staff approached.

On the way inside, Lynn overheard a woman browsing the store with who she assumed was her boyfriend. The woman was looking at items she found interesting, in this case, a small dress. As she held it up to the mirror to imagine herself wearing it, Lynn heard the woman ask him what he thought. The reply made her furious.

"It's ugly, you ugly in anything. Just buy something and let us get going. I got better things to do."

Lynn stormed over to them and introduced herself.

"Hey, excuse me, my name is Lynn. I heard you were looking for an adult opinion… I think the dress looks very good; however,"–Lynn paused and picked up another dress–"This one will go better with your skin tone and hair. It's a little more expensive than the other dress you had picked up, but you are worth it. Don't you think?" She turned, directing the question toward the woman's boyfriend.

"No, this is a complete waste of time. She is a waste of time," the man said flatly.

The woman looked defeated and moved to put the dresses down. Lynn put a hand on her arm to stop her.

"Don't you like these charm bracelets?" Lynn suggested. "They are lovely, but they are over $100. I can't afford that."

Lynn suddenly stepped back onto the man's foot. As he started to cry out in pain, Lynn dug the heel of her shoe straight down onto his foot. He bend over, holding his foot.

"You bloody bitch! Why don't you watch where you are going?!" he screamed.

"Why don't you go? We will look after your girlfriend. She can meet up with you later. Clearly, you don't want to be here," Lynn suggested, as she glanced at the woman.

"I can meet you back at the hotel. You can go be with your friends," the woman stated. "Clearly, they are more important than spending time with me."

The guy stormed out without any hesitation.

"I guess that means I am done shopping; he had all the money," the woman said, with a sad look on her face.

"Don't worry, he will pay," Lynn remarked, holding up his wallet. "I gave him enough money for a ride home," she laughed, with a cheeky smile. "Why do you put up with him?"

"I love him. He didn't always used to treat me like that, just going through a bad time. My name is Courtney; his name is Tom. I'm going to be going back to college in September and I wanted to get some clothes for the new term," Courtney explained, as she shook hands with Lynn.

"This is Ann, my guide around the city. We are about to do some shopping here too. You're welcome to join us." Lynn stated, as she put the charm bracelet on Courtney's wrist.

"Put that on my tab," Lynn said to the store clerk. The staff had been waiting to get started since they arrived; however, they all had to admit, they were proud of how Lynn handled that guy.

Lynn's personal shopping guide took her through all the selections they had to offer. The section labeled "Transitional Investment" caught her eye. Lynn tried on a black badge denim jacket first. Then, she tried on a lightweight double zip jacket. Oh, and a lovely sheer lace bomber jacket with a Japanese dragon design. However, she finally rested on a lace bomber jacket with dark print on the arms and blue color on the middle and back.

To go with it, she picked a sleeveless white textured dress, and a snake sequin mini dress. For accessories, she decided on a leather zip-around backpack. Then, there were mustard-color embroidered Western boots she just had to have. To top things off, Lynn picked a Tree of Life choker and three other necklaces. As Lola was taking care of Ann's and Lynn's tab, Lynn gave Courtney her own money.

Even though Courtney had gotten her boyfriend's wallet, she was too afraid to use any of his money. Therefore, Lynn had given Courtney the money she was planning to use.

Ann had decided the best look for her was in a section called "The Transformative Top." She picked out 2 Batwing V tees, a Palm Mesh bodysuit, 2 white basic ribbed vests, and a beige twist front crop top. She decided to wear the crop top with one of the oversized Batwing V tees.

She allowed the top right side of the top to fall off her right shoulder to give the appearance of exposing her shoulder and the top of her right breast. However, the beige crop top blended in with her skin, hiding it all. The outfit was a perfect tease, and it was cheap too. Ann's long hair hid her bra strap perfectly, so from a distance, it would be impossible to tell that she actually was wearing something underneath her Batwing V tee. It appeared as though she was wearing nothing but the Batwing V tee.

Before they were about to leave, Lynn left a card with her contact information in Courtney's pocket, and they added each other as friends on Facebook. Then Lynn turned to Ann.

"Now, as the boys would say, I am now locked and loaded for action. I feel better now. I look like… Well, like one of you. Let us get something to eat before we head back to Lola," she stated, as she climbed back into the car with Ann.

CHAPTER 3

Target: Lynn (Case:BYGB20984)

"The target is a fourteen year old Caucasian female, currently here in the United States on a study visa. Target graduated high school early. Despite her age, she is incredibly smart and manipulative. She got away with murder and masterminded other petty crimes and organized means to show it to the police.

"This picture is from one of the many admirers of hers, Chris. Right now, she has not committed any crime here in the United States, but we suspect she has come here to learn more than currently offered at the New York State College, trying to expand her C.V.–Sorry, résumé with more things she can get away with.

"She has no siblings. She had one brother, John, who was murdered, and Lynn framed it on her best friend she'd known since elementary. Do not underestimate her. Be on the alert and watch for anything she may be do.
"She currently was last seen over at 5th Avenue in Topshop, and she appears

to have changed her appearance. However, this picture acquired is still the best reference we have, as there was no clear CCTV footage of her at the store.

"The England Police Force would like her in custody. How she is arrested or who by, it does not matter. However, anything that would get her kicked out of the country would be preferred as we would like to deal with our own trash.

"Questions?" Sargent Wilkinson finished, throwing the open question out to everyone present for the briefing.

The room remained silent. Wilkinson turned toward Captain Howard, who then approached him.

"I have received instructions in the spirit of cooperation; we are to assist with this perp in every way possible, as long as it does not affect any of our own cases. I fully understand their need to want to get this person. She made the police over there look stupid. Although many miles away, it's an insult to all law enforcement everywhere, as she will now believe she is above the law."– he paused for a moment and turned to the crowd–"Okay, if nothing else, everyone carry on! Wilkinson in my office! Detective Sarah!" Howard shouted at the end, waving for her to follow him and Wilkinson into his office.

"What's up, Cap'n?" Sarah inquired.

"I need to pair up our exchange student up with you. He has the authority to make arrests, but as he is new, I need him with my best detective, okay?" Howard stated, flirting with the words at the end, hoping the compliment would sweeten the news that he was dumping him with basically what surmounted as a rookie.

"You got it, Cap'n. Come on then, runt. Let's get going, I'm behind already." Sarah turned and left, leaving the door open and Wilkinson standing there with his mouth agape before he was able to say any kind of acknowledgment towards her.

Wilkinson collected himself, and was about to head out the door.

"Wait a minute!" Howard shouted after him.

Wilkinson stopped suddenly and turned towards his captain. Captain Howard leaned over to the desk at his side, used his office keys to unlock the bottom drawer, and pulled out something.

Howard placed a shoulder holster, a police standard issue gun with an ammo clip, and three full stacks of ammo on the table, and pushed it towards Wilkinson.

"Welcome to New York, Sergeant. Your partner will get you licensed up to have and use it. She will take you to the practice range." He gave Wilkinson at serious look.

Again, before Wilkinson could say anything, another shout came from the hall, "You coming, runt?!"

Five minutes later, Wilkinson and Detective Sarah were down in their assigned car, heading over to the police department on 20th Street, coming into the Garment district.

The traffic was congested, but nothing compared to rush hour.

"I see why no one ever drives in this city," Wilkinson said, hoping it would lighten the tension and start a conversation with his new partner, who so far had not said a word to him.

Sarah looked over to him, and responded, "So let us see how good the runt is. Since we are going slower than it would be to walk right now, tell me, what do you see? What do you smell?"

Wilkinson looked to his side and front. He wasn't a cadet fresh out of police training.

"You have food vendors over on the left hand side here. The one selling hot dogs next to the souvenir shop doesn't have a New York license tag. Compared to all the other vendors, I suspect that is a unlicensed hot dog vendor. The people walking on the side walk, half of them look like they are hungover or high," Wilkinson reported.

"Or both," Sarah interrupted. "Go on. What else?"

"Everyone looks tense; they know we are here. So that tells me something around here is or was going on until we showed up," Wilkinson responded, as he turned to face her.

"Not bad. Still doesn't mean you are up to my standards. You want, call it in, so we can get a couple of plain clothes to stay and observe the area after we gone." She handed the radio to him.

As he called it in, Sarah yelled, "Come on!!!"–Sarah blasted the horn– "Should not take thirty minutes to go three fucking miles!!" she screamed, blasting the horn again. "Fuck this," she decided, and pulled over out of the line of traffic, down a side ally onto Golda Meir square and down West 39th St until reaching 5th Avenue.

"Have you ever fired a gun before?" she asked out of the blue. She noticed Wilkinson inspecting the pieces the Captain had given him.

"No, I was not an arms officer. Only used pepper spray and a stun gun. The idea of having and using a gun is kind of intimidating. Is it really needed?" Wilkinson asked.

"Oh, it's needed. Although, what they give us is about as useful as soiled toilet paper, compared to people and armed thugs with shotguns and automatic weapons. Why we carry heavier weapons in the back, plus a few little "knick-knacks" a girl might find useful. Not exactly standard issue, but the Cap'n doesn't ask, so I don't tell," Sarah said, smiling as she pulled out a Desert Eagle from her top, just enough to let him see before slipping it back in place.

"Finally, we are here," she sighed. "Fuck, forty five minutes total. Traffic is getting out of hand these days. Come on, let's go get you legal to use that. They will give you a safety lesson and let you shoot it. And then you be okay to use it. This place has a gun range and what is needed to process rookie cops like you."

The two of them walked around the side to enter into the police entrance instead of the regular public entrance.

"What brings you back to high school, Sarah?" an African American uniformed Sergeant with a heavy Bronx accent questioned. He was six foot one and overweight, with a checkerboard in front of him and three McDonald's bags and a soda cup next to him. His name tag read "Marquis".

"We got an exchange student from across the pond. He got his 'Welcome to New York' care package. Needs to be taught how to tie his shoe laces," she reported, winking at Wilkinson as she provided all the documentation.

"Is it okay if I use my lady to get some practice while I am here?" she requested, patting her chest.

"Sure, the C.O. is not in. You should be good," he responded, as he buzzed her into the range. "Hang-on, sir. Before I let you in, can you put your arm through the window?"

Wilkinson did as requested and Marquis placed a bright pink paper tag around his wrist. "Pink because you're a virgin at this. The Lieutenant will take you and escort you to the safety class."

"How long will all this take?" Wilkinson asked.

"That kind of depends on you and how good you are," Marquis replied, as he buzzed him inside.

Wilkinson had just walked in as the door shut, and he overheard the police radio in Marquis office, "Dispatch 661Alpha Echo: Police presence required. One male deceased by girlfriend's family. Girlfriend's name is Courtney. She is the one who called 911. Shots fired, one casualty."

CHAPTER 4

"So tell me about this person you met at the store?" Lola asked. Lynn was back at Credo's, though the shop was closed with the security blinds drawn shut.

The ceiling lights were on, but everything else was dimmed down, creating minimal lighting just enough to allow each other to see.

"She was with her boyfriend. She was looking at clothes," Lynn replied.

"So what made her stand out to you from the other people in the store?" Lola asked next.

"Someone that has been trampled on most of her life. She had asked her boyfriend for his opinion. His reply infuriated me, but what was worse is she just accepted it. Her self-confidence is shot to the point she calls herself trash, worthless, and she believes it," Lynn replied.

"Okay, this is what I want you to do as your first lesson: become friends with her. I know, I know, you had friends, but not like this. From what you told me, everyone you knew before was expendable to you, a tool. However, Courtney was the first person that stood out to you here, not because of what she could do or how she could be useful, but because of what we all fight against."

"Which is?" Lynn interrupted.

"From becoming like your new friend. To be beaten down to the point one believes they are trash means they had it happen for a long time and not just by her boyfriend. She needs a friend and someone to help her get back up and fight back. You have her on Facebook and you have her number? Ask if she wants to hang out, tonight is still young. I'll have a car ready and you can take her out for a girls night out."—Lola opened up a bag and removed a wallet.—"For you, for tonight; you will need its contents," Lola said, as she handed the black wallet to Lynn, who put it into her purse.

Lynn, as instructed, pulled the card she received from Courtney out of her purse and called the number. At first, a woman answered, identifying herself as Courtney's mother.

"Hello? Courtney's phone. She is busy at the moment. I'm her mom. How can I help?" the woman announced.

"Hey, I am Lynn. I met Courtney at the store earlier and I wanted to know if she like to go out for a girls night?" Lynn paused, as she heard the noise and static of the phone being transferred.

"Yes… hello? This is Courtney." Lynn recognized the next voice that came on the line.

"Hey, it's me from the store earlier. I'm bored and new to the city. I wondered if you want to go out, you could show me about the city at night?" Lynn suggested.

"Err…sure, that would be nice," Courtney replied.

"Okay, if you can give me your add, I have a car that will bring me to yours, and once we pick you up, we can go where you want," Lynn replied, watching Lola nod her approval.

Courtney gave her address and finished, "Call or text to let me know when you are here. I'll be ready for you." Just like that, the call suddenly ended.

"Before you go, remember everything you will need is in that wallet, okay?" Lola pressed.

Lynn retrieved the wallet once again, and as soon as she opened it, she saw what Lola meant. The edge of a New York ID was clearly visible.

"Do I want to know how?" Lynn questioned.

"To be honest, the mundane details would bore you. I still have people in the modeling industry that help out at times. Not every model at shows is always at legal age, so for shows that it is mandated for people to be over twenty one, we make sure our models are ID'd as twenty one year olds," Lola explained. "Now, go on. Go."

The ride took about forty minutes due to the heavy traffic now. It was getting late and both of the New York teams, the Mets and the Yankees, were home tonight, so the city was crowded and alive.

The car entered into Queens, heading for Courtney's address. After the call was made to give Courtney a heads up they were there, Lynn approached the house to knock. The door opened and Courtney's mom greeted her.

"Hello, please come in. She will be ready soon. I'm Courtney's mom. I am so glad she going out. She needs a good night. I been worried about her recently," the woman said quickly with an anxious tone, which was strange as they had just met.

"Should be fun. After I saw her having a hard time at the store, I figured she needed cheering up," Lynn replied.

"What happened at the store?" her mom inquired.

"Her boyfriend gave her a really hard time, calling her ugly when she asked him how she looked. I noticed too while trying on clothes, I saw a lot of bruises and marks on her, hand prints basically," Lynn said, frowning.

"What?! Where?" Courtney's mom exclaimed. Now alert, she looked into another room, which Lynn guessed was the front room, and a man Lynn assumed to be Courtney's dad appeared.

"Hello, I'm her dad. What is this about marks?" he asked as he shook Lynn's hand.

"Yeah, all over her back. I saw them and my guide, Ann, we both saw them. It was quite obvious he has hurt her," Lynn explained, sounding serious.

Courtney's mother turned to her husband and put her hand on his chest to stop him from doing or saying anything more, as Courtney came down the stairs.

"Hey, Lynn, thanks for waiting. I'm ready, let's go." Courtney came sprinting downstairs.

"COME BACK HERE!! I'm not done with you," a male voice roared from behind her.

Courtney made a pleading look at Lynn. "He didn't find your wallet trick funny."

Lynn noticed she was holding her left arm with her right hand. Then the man came bounding down the steps.

"I said come back here! Oh, it's you, bitch. You're lucky I don't call the police on you," he stated sternly.

"Leave it, Tom! Please, I have to go," Courtney pleaded.

"You're not going anywhere with that thing. Why would anyone want to be friends with someone worthless as you?" Tom fired back.

Courtney's dad had heard enough and stormed right up to Tom, pinning him up against the wall.

"You got a nerve to come here and treat her like that," he snarled.

"Courtney, show them your back," Lynn said. She'd had enough of this guy and she knew what to do to end it.

"What? What you talking about.?" Courtney feigned.

Lynn grabbed Courtney's sides, causing her to flinch in pain. Lynn pulled her in front of her mom.

"Lift up her shirt, see for yourself. I suspect he just hurt her arm, why she is holding it," Lynn demanded. Courtney's mom nervously looked down the back of her top.

"Oh love," she sighed, as she lifted up the bottom of Courtney's shirt to reveal her back. Though it didn't look like a back at all, more like she was used as a punching bag.

"Why did you not say anything?" she asked calmly.

"I did that, I fell down the stairs," Courtney protested.

"Just keep your mouth shut, Courtney!" Tom shouted, before her dad punched him, while still pressing his right forearm against Tom's throat, keeping him pinned.

"Why are you protecting him?" Lynn questioned.

"I love him. We are just going through some dark times. It was not always like this, then he changed. It's my fault, so he says. His last girlfriend treated him bad, so he has a hard time trusting women." Courtney said, looking down at the ground.

Suddenly, Tom caught Courtney's dad off guard, punched him, and dove straight for Courtney. He looked like he was going to attack her, so Lynn stepped in front of him and kicked him hard in the lower stomach, just enough to wind him.

Courtney's mom put an arm out and pulled both Lynn and Courtney back behind her. Tom screamed obscenities at them all, demanding Courtney come to him. Courtney made a move to obey him, but was held back by her mom.

Tom took just one more step and suddenly it was all over. There was a loud bang, and Tom dropped to the floor, lifeless and dead.

Forty minutes later, Lola arrived at the home and stood next to Lynn while the police were talking to the family members. Inside the wallet she had given Lynn, she was listed as the emergency contact.

"You certainly don't waste time, do you?" Lola remarked quietly.

"He was a piece of shit. Although, I admit, it went better than I had hoped," Lynn said, just standing and watching over the scene.

"Well, long as she doesn't find out you planned this, I would say you will have a friend. She will feel loyalty once she gets the help. She will see you rescued her from him killing her eventually." Lola placed an arm around Lynn's shoulder.

"There is no reason or excuse for anyone to treat another person as badly as Tom treated Courtney. I cannot believe how devoted to him she was. He had total control over her, abusing her, but she refused to get help because she believed she was not worth saving and because she did love him. Women are only as strong as our weakest link. We need to guard ourselves against predators like him," Lynn stated.

"Well said, Lynn, well said. Oh, if I haven't already said, welcome to New York. You are going to have a lot of fun with what I am going to teach you," Lola said, as they both climbed into the car and drove away.